LTL

ALLEN COUNTY PUBLIC LIBRARY

3 1833 04218 3324

D1093000

Bedtime Prayers

Written and compiled by Christine Wright
Illustrated by Roma Bishop

BAKER
A DIVISION OF
Baker Book House Co

Allen County Public Library

My home

At home

At home I have my own bed,
My own place to sit,
My own toys and clothes,
And everyone knows my name!
That's why it's nice being at home.
A great big thank you
From me to you, loving God, for my home.

Where I live

Thank you, Lord God,
For the place where I live,
For the park and the swings and the slide,
For the houses, the shops,
For the cars in the street,
And especially for all of the people we meet.
Thank you, Lord God,
For the place where I live.

Digging in the garden

Father God, today I helped with the digging.
We dug, dug, dug with a great big spade,
And worms and millipedes came out to play.
We snipped at the stalks and branches and leaves,
And shook all the seedpods and saw tiny seeds.
Now it's up to you, God.
Only you can make plants grow, grow, GROW!

People who love me

God our Father,
Thank you for people who love me.
There are sisters and brothers,
Fathers and mothers,
Cousins, uncles, and aunts.
There are grandmas and grandads,
Daughters and sons.
Grown-ups and children,
Tall people and short ones,
Old people and young ones.
And people in between.
Thank you for my special family.
Father of us all,
You love us, every one.

Looking after pets

Cats like sleeping all curled up,
And dogs enjoy a walk.
Hamsters need a place to play
And parrots like to talk.
Every pet, small or big,
Needs someone to care for it.
Lord Jesus, you know how to care and be kind.
Teach me how to look after my pets
So that they are happy living with us.

I got cross

Dear Jesus,
I got cross today.
Everything went wrong.
I don't like being cross.
It makes me unhappy
And people get cross with me.
I am sorry now.
I need a hug,
Then I'll be happy again.

Playtime

When I grow up

I want to *be*

... a fireman.

... or a farmer on a tractor.

... or a postman with a bag of letters.

... or an astronaut way out in space.

... or a cook in a kitchen.

... or a doctor making people *better*.

Dear God, thank you for all the things I can *be*.

Playing with friends

Out to play
This sunny day
We ran and ran
Together.

It was such fun
Out in the sun
We shouted and laughed
Together.

Thank you, God,
For all my friends.

Everyone's different

Jesus, my friend,
I'm glad you make everyone different.
Some are good at cooking
And make yummy meals to eat.
Some are good at music
And make up songs to sing.
Some can paint and some can draw
—everyone's good at something!

Thank you for everything I love doing
And for the special things I can do for you.

Making cakes

Dear God, today we made cakes.
I love the stirring and mixing,
The beating and scraping,
But best of all, the licking!
Thank you, God, for the taste of cakes.

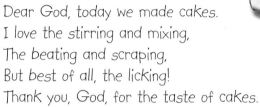

Sharing

Dear God,
Help me to share my toys with my friends.
Sometimes I don't want to share,
And we have arguments.
I'm sorry I got cross with my friend today.

All my toys

Dear God,
I'm thinking about all my toys...
Here's my cuddly teddy bear,
There's my big, blue ball,
On the floor a box of bricks,
My drawing on the wall,
Jigsaw puzzles, a picture book—
Which toys are most fun?
Thank you for all the toys I have.
Thank you for every one.

So many different toys

Look at all the toys I have!
Toys that pop up, toys that move,
Toys I can push and toys I can pull,
Toys that can squeak, toys that can talk,
Toys I can build with, toys that can walk,
Toys I can share, and toys that can fly,
Toys I can cuddle, toys that can nod,
For all these toys, I thank you, God.

Out and about

The sea and the sky

Splashy sea,
Big blue sky,
Shiny stones,
Grasses tall.
Trickling sand,
Knobbly shells...

Thank you, God!
You made it all.

The seaside

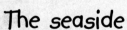

Down by the sea
Where the waves crash in,
There are shells in the sand,
That the water brings in.

Lord, you made the seaside,
You made the sand and shells,
The seagull's cry, each wave's white crest,
Wild wind and salty smell.

Outdoors

Lord God,
I like to run around outdoors.
Picnics and puddles,
See-saws and swings,
Flowers and green grass
Rainbows and things...
And you made them all.
Hooray for outdoors!

A windy day

Today the wind was blowing!
I felt it on my face.
I heard the rushing sound it made,
My hair blew out of place.
Dear God, I love a windy day!
It makes me want to run,
to laugh and shout
With my arms stretched out.
Thank you, God, it's fun!

Happy times

I know you're there, Jesus,
In happy times,
When I'm smiling,
Having fun.
I'm happy now, dear Jesus.
Be here with me now!

Sad times

I know you're there, Jesus,
In sad times,
When I'm crying,
When I'm scared.
I'm sad now, dear Jesus.
Be here with me now.

Out and about

Animals and birds

I love animals.
Thank you, God!
Soft and silky ones,
Gruff and licky ones,
Smooth and slithery ones,
Whiskery, frisky ones.
Animals are fun.

I love birds.
Thank you, God!
Tweety and cheepy ones,
Hopping and flappy ones,
Hooting and feathery ones,
Pecking and scratchy ones.
Birds are fun!

Getting lost

Loving God, when I'm out and about,
Please keep me safe,
Because it's no fun being lost.
Help me to keep hold of Mom's hand
Or stay close to Dad.
Then they'll know where I am
And I'll know where they are.

The world around us

The seasons

Spring...

Trees sprout bright green leaves,
Shoots come up in empty earth,
Bright flowers are peeping out,
Birds begin to sing and shout.
Suddenly the world is fun,
And everyone enjoys the sun.

God, you made it. God, you gave it.
Thank you for it, thank you for it!

Summer...

Blue skies, sunny days,
Warm sunshine, foamy waves,
Cool ice-cream, happy faces,
Rustling leaves in breezy places.
Buzzing bees on bright new flowers,
Sudden clouds bring sudden showers.
It's summer time!

God, you made it. God, you gave it.
Thank you for it, thank you for it!

Autumn...

Red leaves, yellow leaves,
Orange leaves, brown leaves,
Crunchy leaves, swirling leaves,
Running-along-the ground leaves,
Deep leaves, piles of leaves,
Let me jump in them, please!

God, you made it.
 God, you gave it.
   Thank you for it,
      thank you for it!

Winter...

Boots on, gloves on,
Hats on and coats on.

Autumn's gone,
Winter's here, lots of fun!

God, you made it. God, you gave it.
Thank you for it, thank you for it!

The sky

Creator God,
The sky does something I can't do!
It changes color from gray to blue.
It's pink in the morning and deep blue at night,
And when the sun shines, it's beautifully bright.
When I look at the sky, I know that it's true:
There really is no one as clever as you!
Thank you for the sky.

Tiny creatures

Thank you, God, for making tiny creatures
That crawl and creep and slither and slide.
Thank you for sea spiders and starfish,
For snails and mollusks,
Scallops, cockles, and crabs.
Help us to look after the world you have made.

Creepy crawlies

Spotty ladybirds, stripy snails,
Tiny spiders, buzzing bees,
Slimy slugs with silvery trails,
Wiggly worms and centipedes,
Crawling creatures with long tails:
Thank you, God, you made all these.

Good things to eat

The food you bring me

Where does my food come from?
Farmers
Grew it in their fields.
Truck drivers
Took it to the factories.
Factory workers
Packed it and sent it to the stores.
Grocers
Stacked it on the shelves.
We bought it and brought
it home.

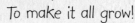

Someone
Cooked it and put it on my plate.
So much work to
Make food for me—
Thank you, God, for all those people.
Thank you, God, for rain and sunshine
To make it all grow!

Hungry people

Loving God, it's so sad:
Some people don't have enough to eat.
Help us to remember them and pray for them
When we eat our meals.
Show us a way to help them
Have the food they need.

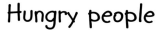

Food

Dear God, thank you for food to eat.
Thank you for making fruit,
Sweet and juicy, crisp and crunchy.
Thank you for vegetables,
Lots of different colors and shapes.
I like bread to eat. I like pasta.
Thank you for milk to drink,
And for cheese and chocolate and chips!
Thank you for yummy yogurt!
Thank you, God, for the sun and the rain
That helps my food grow.
Thank you, God, for food to eat.

Shopping

Dear God, we did a lot of shopping today:
Huge brown potatoes,
Shiny green pepper,
Bendy yellow bananas,
Crusty white bread,
Six brown eggs,
Ripe red tomatoes.
What a lot of things you have made!
Thank you for shops and for so much to choose from.

Ice cream

So cold as it touches my lips.
So soft as it melts in my mouth.
So sweet as it tingles my tongue.
So cool as it slides down my throat
And when it's inside my tummy,
Another spoonful please!
Ice cream is lovely.
Thank you, God, for ice cream to eat.

Good things to eat

In the Kitchen

When I'm hungry
The kitchen smells great!
What's cooking?
Pasta bubbling in the pan?
Chips sizzling, beans bubbling?
Pie or pizza, sweet corn, peas?
Rice fluffing in steaming water?
Fish fingers almost done?
Thank you, Lord, for good food.
I'm never hungry for too long.

Thank you for bread

I like bread.
It smells so good.
Yummy, yummy,
Rub my tummy!
Thank you, God, for bread.

I like bread.
It tastes so good.
Crunchy, munchy,
Eat for lunchy!
Thank you, God, for bread.

I like bread.
It looks so good.
Slice by slicey,
Buttered nicely.
Thank you, God, for bread.

Special days

Christmas

I'm tingly and excited.
I simply can't keep quiet.
Today has been so busy
From morning until night.
It's Christmas!
It's Christmas!
Christmas is here again!
Christmas is full of wonders
It's sparkly and bright
To help us all remember
Who was born
On Christmas night.
God gave us baby Jesus,
Born as a little boy.
A special kind of present
Who came to bring us joy.

I'm tingly and excited.
But now it's time to rest.
Dear God, help me remember
That your present is the best.
It's Christmas!
It's Christmas!
Christmas is here again!

A new baby

Tiny nose,
Tiny ears,
Little eyes,
Little mouth.
Thank you, Jesus,
Our new baby is born!
Small fingers,
Small toes,
Teeny body,
Teeny head.
Thank you, Jesus.
I'm giving our new baby
A big, BIG welcome.

Sundays

Thank you, Jesus, for Sundays—
A special day for you.
We go to church with our family,
And meet to worship you.
Praising you, stories too,
Sing and pray, a special day.
Meet our friends, games to play,
I'm sad when it ends,
Your special day.

Easter day

Jesus, the saddest day of all
Is the story of how you died.
But the best story in the world
Is the story of you coming alive!

Special days

Every day and night

Every day is special
When we spend it, Lord, with you.
Each day can be wonderful
And every night can, too.
Jesus, bless my family,
And help us day by day
To be kinder to each other,
More like you in every way.

My birthday

Birthdays are brilliant
With presents and parties
And a cake on the table for tea,
All for a special birthday person.
Today that person is me!

Thank you, God, for my special day.
And thank you for everyone
Who gave me such a happy time.
Please bless them, every one.

Bedtime

 ## Today

Thank you for today, dear God:
For the food I ate,
For the clothes I wore,
For the friends I played with,
For the fun we had.
Thank you, God, for everything.

Bedtime

Yawn, yawn,
I'm sleepy now.
Time to snuggle into bed.

Ho hum,
And close my eyes.
Time to rest my tired head.

Dear God,
You know best.
A time to play and a time to rest.
Good night!

A blessing

Please, God,
Bless me when I'm walking,
Bless me when I'm talking,
Bless me when I'm playing,
Bless me when I'm praying,
Bless me when I'm eating,
Bless me when I'm sleeping.
Please bless me every minute
Of the day and night.

Be near me

Be near me, Lord Jesus,
I ask you to stay
Close by me for ever,
And love me, I pray.
Bless all the dear children
In your tender care,
And fit us for heaven
To live with you there.

Text copyright © 2002 Christine Wright
Illustrations copyright © 2002 Roma Bishop
Copyright © 2002 AD Publishing Services Ltd
1 Churchgates, The Wilderness, Berkhamsted, Herts

Published by Baker Books
a division of Baker Books House Company
P.O. Box 6287, Grand Rapids, MI49516-6287
ISBN 0-8010-1226-0

First published 2002 by AD Publishing Services Ltd.

Library of Congress Cataloging-in-Publication data is on file at the
Library of Congress in Washington, D.C.

All rights reserved. No part of this publication may be reproduced or
transmitted in any form or by any means, electronic or mechanical,
including photocopying, recording or any information storage and
retrieval system, without either prior permission in writing from the
publisher or a licence permitting restricted copying.

Printed and bound in Spain.

For current information about all releases from Baker Book House,
visit our web site: http://www.bakerbooks.com